# Mr Badger
## and the
# Big Surprise

Leigh Hobbs

ALLEN&UNWIN

*For Jack Hobbs*

First published in 2010

Copyright © Leigh Hobbs 2010

Cataloguing-in-Publication details are available from the
National Library of Australia www.trove.nla.gov.au

ISBN 978 1 74237 417 8

Cover and text design by Sandra Nobes
Set in 15 pt Cochin by Sandra Nobes
Author photograph by Peter Gray
This book was printed in May 2014 at McPherson's Printing Group,
76 Nelson St, Maryborough, Victoria 3465, Australia.
www.mcphersonsprinting.com.au

7 9 10 8

MIX
Paper from
responsible sources
FSC
www.fsc.org    FSC® C001695

The paper in this book is FSC® certified.
FSC® promotes environmentally responsible,
socially beneficial and economically viable
management of the world's forests.

# Contents

*Mr Badger's house in Mayfair.*

# CHAPTER 1

## Behind the Hedge

Mr Badger lives in Mayfair. However, if you ever find yourself in this part of central London, I wouldn't bother searching for Mr Badger's house. People have walked past it every day for years without even noticing it.

So I shall describe it for you.

Mr Badger's house is quite small and has a thatched roof.

The front door is light blue with a small window and pink-and-cream spotted curtains. On either side of the door are bigger windows which, at night when the inside lights are on, could give the impression that this house has eyes.

Not that you can see them, because
Mr Badger's house sits behind a thick
hedge that hides it from the busy street.

In the morning, it is usually still dark when Mr Badger leaves for work.

He takes care to lift the latch of the faded picket gate very quietly, so as not to wake anyone up.

In the evening, it is almost always dark when he arrives home again with a copy of the afternoon paper tucked under his arm.

# CHAPTER 2

## The Walk to Work

One morning, not so very long ago, Mr Badger set off for work even earlier than usual.

Every day was a busy day for Mr Badger but this particular day promised to be busier than most, for it was a rather special day, in more ways than one.

On his way to work, Mr Badger liked looking at all his favourite places – the interesting old houses, pretty arcades, art galleries and tea shops that could be found in this part of London. He sometimes paused to glance inside the elegantly lit entrance foyers of smart flats and hotels, where just about everyone was still sleeping.

Not everyone was asleep, though. Other early risers were already at work. Mrs Mopptop, for instance, was busy arranging fresh flowers inside the entrance to Lady Camilla Feather's very grand home when Mr Badger passed by. As usual, they gave each other a friendly wave.

As he neared the Empire Tea Shop, Mr Badger looked left and right then crossed the street. He strode up some big stone steps covered with crimson carpet. Large brass doors at the top made a lovely swishing sound as they were pushed open.

'Good morning, Mr Badger!' said
Harry the doorman.

'Good morning to you, Harry,'
said Mr Badger.

As always, Mr Badger looked absolutely splendid in his pale-blue waistcoat, butter-yellow bow-tie, bright-red tail coat, black pinstriped trousers and very shiny shoes.

He strolled along the corridor beneath the chandeliers towards his office, his paws in their white gloves tucked behind his back.

CHAPTER 3

# A Busy Day for Mr Badger

Mr Badger is the Special Events Manager at the Boubles Grand Hotel (pronounced *Boublay*). He is in charge of parties, weddings, balls – well, anything really that one might call a special occasion.

Mr Badger has worked there for years. So did his father, and Grandfather Badger before him.

On this particular day, Mr Badger had a very important party to organise. It was a birthday party with hundreds of guests, mountains of food, a little orchestra, party games and a giant birthday cake.

*Miss Pims.*

Fortunately he didn't have to do all the work himself. Mr Badger had a wonderful helper – a personal assistant called Miss Pims. They had worked together for quite a long time.

16

*Mr Badger and Miss Pims worked well as a team.*

'How are we this morning,
Miss Pims?' said Mr Badger.

'Raring to go, Mr Badger,' replied
Miss Pims. 'We certainly have a big day
ahead of us.'

'And don't I know it,' said Mr Badger,
giving his glasses a careful wipe.

Sylvia Smothers-Carruthers was the birthday girl, and she was turning seven.

Her grandparents, Sir Cecil and Lady Celia Smothers-Carruthers, were the owners of the Boubles Grand Hotel. They were hosting the party, and they wanted everything to be perfect for their sweet little Sylvia.

*Sir Cecil and Lady Celia Smothers-Carruthers weren't just grandparents, they were* grand *grandparents.*

Sir Cecil and Lady Celia Smothers-Carruthers were rather old and their hearing wasn't nearly as good as it had been. Nor was their eyesight. That might explain why they often didn't notice when their dear little Sylvia was not as nicely behaved as they would have liked.

Sylvia was *very* fussy. She wanted her seventh birthday to be a party that she and her friends would never forget. Sylvia had no idea that her wish was about to come true.

Mr Badger and Miss Pims had carefully calculated what would be required for the party: 410 watercress sandwiches, 820 party pies, 512 butterfly cakes with pink-and-yellow icing, five large tubs of chocolate mousse, two tubs of vanilla ice-cream and six large tubs of strawberry sorbet, seven assorted sponge cakes – not counting the giant birthday cake and the layered sponge fingers – plus

fourteen huge bowls of strawberry jelly
with raspberries and cream, and of
course the three dozen pineapple tartlets,
which were Sylvia's personal favourites.

Sylvia Smothers-Carruthers' closest
205 friends had been invited to the party.

Mr Badger knew from past
experience what big appetites little
children often have.

Even though Sylvia already
had everything money could buy, the
invitation had said in great big letters:
'DO NOT FORGET TO BRING A
PRESENT!' It also said: 'Do not dress
up too much.'

There was a not-so-secret reason
for this, which was that Sylvia was
planning to wear her best party frock
and didn't want anyone else to look
better than *she* did.

This was one of the many reasons
why Sylvia was known by quite a few
of her 205 friends – no, in fact *all* of her
friends – as Sylvia Smartypants.

# ❧ **INVITATION** ❧

You are invited to a party at...

## THE
## BOUBLES GRAND HOTEL

to celebrate the seventh birthday of the
wonderful and very special...

*Sylvia Smothers – Carruthers*

1. ## DO NOT FORGET
   ## TO BRING A PRESENT !

2. ## DO NOT DRESS UP TOO MUCH!

*Signed...* **Sylvia**

Details on back...make sure you look...!

## CHAPTER 4

# The Guests Arrive

Mr Badger had worked late for weeks and weeks – planning, checking and re-checking all the party details to ensure that Sylvia's special day would run smoothly, without any nasty incidents.

Now, everything was ready in the
Boubles Grand Hotel Ballroom.

The tables were laid and the gleam
of silver knives, forks and spoons on
the pale-pink tablecloths, together with

all the beautiful plates on which was
written 'BOUBLES GRAND HOTEL',
made a truly wonderful spectacle.

The Boubles Grand Hotel Orchestra
had practised 'Happy Birthday' twenty-
five or maybe even twenty-six times.

Pretty pink, blue and yellow balloons hovered in the air, and coloured streamers dangled from the ornate ceiling.

'I must say, it looks splendid, doesn't it!' whispered Mr Badger to Miss Pims.

'Stunning,' replied Miss Pims with a little nod and a big grin.

Mr Badger watched as the guests arrived. They came up the stairs and through the swishing doors at the grand entrance.

Sylvia's guests gazed in amazement at the high ceilings held up by pink-and-green marble columns.

And everyone stopped to look
at Algernon, the ancient-looking ape
standing in a glass case in the foyer.
Algernon had lived to a ripe old age.
He had been a close friend of Sir Cecil
Smothers-Carruthers, whose family
had founded the Boubles Grand Hotel
a long time ago. But that's another story.

It was beginning to look like the children had ignored one of Sylvia's important instructions. The girls were all in their finest party frocks, and the boys, too, had gone to a lot of trouble with their appearance.

Of course this was completely understandable. After all, the party *was* in the Boubles Grand Hotel Ballroom.

Every guest was carrying a gift. Some gifts were so large that only a small pair of legs could be seen staggering towards the table set up especially for Sylvia's birthday presents.

Soon 205 little guests and nearly as many parents stood excitedly on either side of a long red carpet, ready to welcome in the birthday girl. All eyes were facing the big double doors at the front of the ballroom, through which, very soon, Sylvia Smothers-Carruthers would be making her great big entrance.

# CHAPTER 5

## The Big Entrance

Part of Mr Badger's job was to make announcements at special occasions, and Sylvia's birthday party was definitely one of those.

He rang a little bell, cleared his throat and waited for silence.

'Ladies, gentlemen and birthday guests all. On behalf of Sir Cecil and Lady Celia Smothers-Carruthers and the Boubles Grand Hotel, I wish to welcome you to the celebration of Sylvia Smothers-Carruthers' seventh birthday.'

*Mr Badger liked to welcome the hotel guests.*

Mr Badger was good at this sort of thing. He'd learnt a lot about making announcements from his father. Actually, his father had taught him almost everything he knew about the Boubles Grand Hotel and how it worked.

With a swish and a flourish, in came
Sylvia Smothers-Carruthers, escorted
by her loving grandparents.

Sylvia made quite an entrance.
She was wearing a very frilly pink
dress with lots of bows and feathers.

*Sylvia thought she was special, very special.*

It was obvious by the way she walked that Sylvia thought of herself as a little princess.

Suddenly there was a crash and a loud bang. All eyes turned to the back of the ballroom. Someone, no doubt momentarily dazzled by the blinding sparkles in Sylvia's costume, had tripped and knocked over the table laden with Sylvia's birthday presents.

Sylvia was furious.

Of course it was an accident and of course they hadn't meant it, but that made no difference to Sylvia Smothers-Carruthers.

As far as she was concerned, her big birthday entrance was ruined.

Sylvia shrieked and stamped and threw herself on the shiny parquet floor.

She looked a little – in fact, she looked a lot – like a badly behaved tangle of bright-pink fairy floss.

Without any fuss, Mr Badger calmly
motioned to Miss Pims, and in no time
at all everything was back in its place
and Sylvia's presents were once more
carefully arranged on the table ready
for her to open.

The party was about to begin.

## CHAPTER 6

# Mr Badger Saves the Day

With a click of his paws,
Mr Badger signalled for the
orchestra to start playing. Soon
the noise of Sylvia's tantrum was
completely drowned out by music,
laughter and merry chatter.

All these happy sounds prompted
Mr Badger to look around the room,
past the guests, until his eyes caught
a reflection – his own – in one of the
many ornate mirrors.

Many years ago he had gazed into
that very same mirror, but the reflection
back then had been of a much younger,
smaller Mr Badger, standing in front
of his father.

Bending down, his father had gently straightened little Mr Badger's bow-tie and helped him to put on his own pair of crisp, white gloves.

Then they had stepped back to check
their matching uniforms before trotting
off to help serve afternoon tea in the
Grand Ballroom.

You see, Mr Badger's father had
been Head Waiter at the Boubles
Grand Hotel. Sometimes on weekends,
and often at holiday time, he would
take his boy to work with him. Young
Mr Badger had adored spending time
with his father.

No wonder Mr Badger loved his
job. Every part of the hotel was full of
happy memories.

Mr Badger was jolted back to the present by a dreadful commotion.

Sylvia Smothers-Carruthers had leapt up onto the gift table and was ripping open her presents.

Not just with her hands. She was using her teeth as well.

'Good heavens, my dear,' said Lady Celia Smothers-Carruthers. She leant over and gently suggested to Sylvia that it might be nice to read the cards with their thoughtful birthday wishes first.

Sylvia let out a loud sigh and, curling her lip, proceeded to pretend to read all of the cards at once – most of them upside down or sideways.

It must be said that Sylvia didn't look very impressed with her gifts. Rudely, she failed to even try to hide her disappointment.

Mr Badger was eager for the party to proceed as planned – there was a very full program of games and activities to come. So he quickly removed the mess of paper and ribbons and helped Sylvia down from the table into the arms of her grandparents.

Luckily the orchestra was ready to strike up the first notes for a lively game of musical chairs.

Sadly, this wasn't a great success, for every time the orchestra stopped and there was a mad scramble for the chairs, Sylvia missed out on a seat.

Many a guest was wrestled to the floor when Sylvia insisted that a seat be hers. Unfortunately Sylvia's behaviour got worse rather than better as her party progressed. In the end, Mr Badger followed Sylvia around the ballroom with a spare chair.

## CHAPTER 7

# The Birthday Girl's
# Big Moment

Now the most thrilling moment of Sylvia's party had arrived.

Mr Badger clicked his paws once more. The lights dimmed and, after a loud clang from the cymbals and a blast from two trumpets, Miss Pims wheeled in Sylvia's splendid big birthday cake, candles ablaze. It was an extravaganza.

Sylvia had insisted there be a hundred candles on her cake. Not that she was turning a hundred years old, of course – as everyone knew, she was in fact turning seven. But Sylvia had wanted a hundred candles on her cake so that it would look spectacular.

It *certainly* did. As well as the candles, there were four layers and nine different types of icing.

In the near dark, ringed with feathers and sparkles, Sylvia's face glowed from the light of the candles as the guests sang 'Happy Birthday'.

Now it was time for Sylvia to blow out the candles and make a wish. The room was absolutely quiet as she climbed onto a cushion on top of a chair, took a deep breath, and…and… and…sneezed!

There was a whoosh of air and a flash of light as a hundred candles went out – all at once. The Boubles Grand Hotel Ballroom was plunged into darkness.

When the lights came back on, Sylvia's guests gasped. The birthday girl's face was covered with black soot from the candles and fairy dust from her fancy frock. Worse still, many of the feathers on Sylvia's dress had been blown off, and those that hadn't were sticking out in all directions.

Sylvia looked a fright.

Poor Sylvia, her cake was all but destroyed. But Mr Badger knew how important it was for the birthday girl to make a wish, so he sent Miss Pims to the kitchen to collect a spare, not-so-grand cake and thereby saved Sylvia's special day.

After she'd made her wish, Sylvia was led away by Miss Pims to be cleaned up.

The party had been a great success – well, certainly one to remember.

Sylvia's guests had all had a wonderful time. And so in fact had Sylvia, for she had managed to stay the centre of attention most of the time.

Sylvia was looking forward to her eighth birthday party already (and so were her guests). However, her grandparents weren't quite so keen.

## CHAPTER 8

# Goodnight, Mr Badger

It was late by the time Mr Badger had personally farewelled Sir Cecil and Lady Celia Smothers-Carruthers and little Sylvia. Not forgetting her 205 friends and their parents.

Sylvia's presents had been loaded into a Boubles Grand Hotel delivery van and were already on their way to Sylvia's home.

In the ballroom, Mr Badger swung into action. There was a big mess to be

tidied up, not that there was much food
or drink left. In fact, looking around,
Mr Badger realised there was none.

Every last glass of pink lemonade had been drunk. And every one of those delicious 410 watercress sandwiches, 820 party pies, 512 butterfly cakes, seven sponge cakes, eight tubs of assorted ice-cream, five tubs of mousse, huge bowls of strawberry jelly with raspberries and cream, and layered sponge fingers had been eaten by Sylvia, her hungry little friends and their parents.

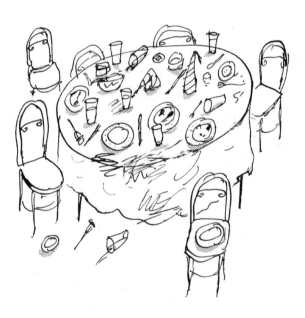

There was certainly not one pineapple tartlet to be seen. Sylvia had hidden these away amongst her pile of presents right at the beginning of the party.

What's more, every last piece of birthday cake had been eaten. All gone without a trace.

*Mr Badger and Miss Pims organised the clean-up as usual.*

The tables were cleared, the beautiful Boubles cutlery and china plates washed, dried and stacked away for the next party or special event. The pretty pink tablecloths, now covered with cake and watercress sandwich crumbs and jelly splodges, had been gathered up and sent down to the hotel laundry.

The balloons had long since disappeared, and all the coloured streamers had been taken down from the ceiling.

Miss Pims had gone, and the ballroom was all quiet and clean, as if the party had never happened.

Even the members of the Boubles
Grand Hotel Orchestra were now home,
no doubt enjoying a well-earned sleep.

In fact, absolutely nothing remained
of Sylvia Smothers-Carruthers' seventh
birthday party.

'Never mind,' sighed Mr Badger.

It was time for him to go home, too.

# CHAPTER 9

# Mr Badger's Secret

But tonight was not just any night, and today had not been just any day. For today was Mr Badger's birthday. And now as he gazed about the ballroom, Mr Badger remembered how, long ago, he had spent his own seventh birthday at the Boubles Grand Hotel.

On that day, for a special treat, young Mr Badger had been taken to one of the Boubles Grand Hotel kitchens to watch his grandfather the chef decorate a beautiful big birthday cake, which he had baked especially for his beloved grandson...Mr Badger.

A little later, however, there had been a disaster in the dining room. At a birthday party for another little boy turning seven on that same day, the birthday boy's cake had been knocked off the table and onto the floor.

Mr Badger's father had replaced the ruined cake with his little son's special one. Yes, the very one created by his grandfather. Terrible but true – but Mr Badger's father had had no choice.

This was a memory that had stayed with Mr Badger, ever since he was very small.

On his way home, as Mr Badger walked quietly past a shop window, he noticed the reflection of a tear. It was running down his cheek.

Mr Badger hadn't mentioned
to anyone that it was his birthday.
He was far too proud and professional
and grown-up for that.

However, he had *rather* hoped that
at least one piece of Sylvia Smothers-
Carruthers' birthday cake might have
been left uneaten.

The walk home seemed especially
long that night.

# CHAPTER 10

## Bravo, Mr Badger

It was freezing cold and nearly midnight by the time Mr Badger lifted the latch, opened the picket gate and walked up the path to his front door.

*This had been a special day for Mr Badger.*

It was quiet, very quiet, as he reached for the key. Mr Badger stepped into a darkened room, fumbling for the light switch.

But this was not just any night. Mr Badger was in for a big surprise.

For when he turned on the light, he saw that the sitting room was full of balloons and coloured streamers.

Many bright and eager faces were beaming up at him.

Why, there was Mrs Badger, with their darling daughter Berenice, and of course baby Badger, too. Mrs Mopptop, Miss Pims, Harry the doorman – in fact, all of Mr Badger's friends from the Boubles Grand Hotel – were there as well.

*What a welcome, thought Mr Badger.*

Everyone cheered and cried,
'Surprise!'

And so it was.

Mr Badger's birthday hadn't been
forgotten after all.

On the table lay a stack of plates,
spoons, forks and, best of all, a splendid
big birthday cake with letters in
beautiful pink icing that said: 'Happy
Birthday, Mr Badger!'

'Oh my goodness!' said a most surprised Mr Badger. In fact, he could barely speak.

Once again a little tear ran down his cheek.

But this time, it was a very happy one.

The End

More Leigh Hobbs books for you
to enjoy from Allen & Unwin

*Horrible Harriet*
*Hooray for Horrible Harriet*
*4F for Freaks*
*Freaks Ahoy*
*Old Tom's Big Book of Beauty*
*Mr Chicken Goes to Paris*
and of course the Mr Badger books

For more details, visit Leigh's website:
**www.leighhobbs.com.au**

Collect all of Mr Badger's adventures
at the Boubles Grand Hotel.

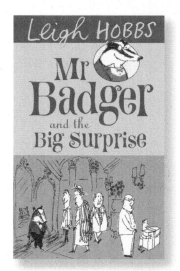

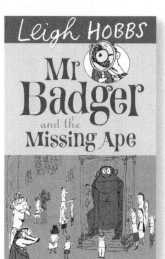

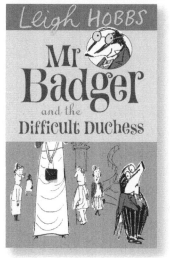

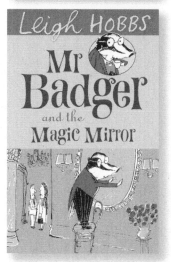

## *A Bit about the Author*

Leigh Hobbs was born in Melbourne. He grew
up in Bairnsdale, with a complete lack of interest
and talent in sport and maths, but loving art right
from the start. In fact, he enthusiastically drew every
day, before and after school, using a drawing board
made by his father.

That board is still in regular use, though now
it is covered with over fifty years' worth of scribble,
most of it made by a pen dipped in black ink,
always Leigh's favourite drawing medium.

Another constant in Leigh's life is his fascination
with history, English history in particular.
He finds London a source of endless interest
and visits regularly, studying favourite sights
and searching for new ones.